Snow White

An Islamic Tale

In the name of Allah, the One God, the Most Compassionate, the Most Merciful

To my parents-in-law, Judy Arleen Kayden and Terry Lee Kayden,
who never tire of illuminating the world with their generosity and kindness. I love you.
F. G.

Snow White: An Islamic Tale

Published by
THE ISLAMIC FOUNDATION
Markfield Conference Centre, Ratby Lane, Markfield
Leicestershire, LE67 9SY, United Kingdom
E-mail: publications@islamic-foundation.com Website: www.islamic-foundation.com

Distributed by
KUBE PUBLISHING LTD
Tel +44 (01530) 249230, Fax +44 (01530) 249656
E-mail: info@kubepublishing.com Website: www.kubepublishing.com

3rd impression, 2016

Author Fawzia Gilani
Cover and Book Illustrations Shireen Adams
Book design Nasir Cadir
Editor Yosef Smyth and Fatima D'Oyen

A Cataloguing-in-Publication Data record for this book is available from the British Library

ISBN 978-0-86037-526-5

Printed by Imak Ofset, Turkey

Snow White
An Islamic Tale

FAWZIA GILANI

Illustrated by SHIREEN ADAMS

Once upon a time there lived an honest and rich merchant who had a kind-hearted wife. Their only sadness was that they didn't have a child.

One winter's day, as the snow fell gently, the merchant's wife sat by a window reading the Qur'an. Suddenly she felt very tired and fell asleep. In her dream she saw a little girl playing. As soon as the merchant's wife awoke, she made a *du'a.* "Dear Allah," she said, "please bless me with a daughter who is as patient as Job, as peaceful as dawn, with a heart as pure as snow."

A year later the merchant's wife had a baby daughter. The wife remembered her dream on the snowy day, so she named the child Snow White. As the child grew her parents brought many teachers to educate her. She learnt about Islam, science, language and played sports. One day, her mother gave her a gift of a Qur'an, "My sweet child," she said, "always keep this close to you. May Allah bless you with patience, peace and purity."

Sadly, Snow White's mother fell ill and died when she was ten. The little girl and her father were heartbroken. It was all they could do to ask Allah to give them patience and strength.

Snow White took great comfort in the words of the Qur'an and her prayers. At times she missed her mother very much. This worried the merchant greatly so he decided to marry thinking that Snow White would be happier if she had the love of a mother again.

The merchant's new wife was very beautiful. At first she behaved affectionately towards Snow White. She appeared to be concerned with prayer and charity but eventually it all stopped.
The stepmother was very vain. She was constantly adorning herself, changing from one costume to another and admiring herself in the many mirrors she surrounded herself with. Rather than caring for Snow White, the stepmother demanded that the child prepare all the meals, wash the clothes and clean the house. It greatly angered and saddened the merchant to see his young daughter being mistreated and neglected, so one day he complained to the stepmother.

It was shortly after this that the merchant died of a strange illness. Sadness filled the poor orphan's heart. She tried to console herself with the story of Prophet Job. Many tears were shed as Snow White spent her nights in prayer.

Now that the merchant was gone, the stepmother began to do many horrid and dreadful things. If she saw something she liked, she would take it by force, whether it was from a child or an elder. And it was common for people to mysteriously disappear if she disliked something they said or did.

It came to be known that the stepmother practiced magic. At night strange words could be heard from her room followed by a loud and wicked cackle. Poor Snow White would shake in her bed and remember the verse in the Qur'an about those who studied magic,

> *And they learned what harmed them, not what profited them. And they knew that the buyers of (magic) would have no share in the happiness of the Hereafter.*[1]

The stepmother also owned a *jinn,* which would answer all her questions. She would say to the *jinn,* "*Jinn, jinn,* obey my call. Who is the fairest of them all?"
The *jinn* would reply, "O Lady, you are beautiful, fine and fair. To you there is no other who does compare."

Whenever the stepmother asked the *jinn* who the most beautiful was, he would always give the same answer. She was so vain and so jealous that she couldn't abide anyone being more beautiful than her.

One day the stepmother said to the *jinn,* "*Jinn, jinn,* obey my call. Who is the fairest of them all?"
But to her shock the *jinn* replied, "O Lady, you were once fair, 'tis true, but now Snow White is fairer than you."
On hearing this, the stepmother flew into a rage, screaming and ranting.
"There is no one fairer than me! No one!" she shrieked.
The stepmother stamped her foot on the ground and waved her fists in the air. She picked up a chair and threw it against a wall. Her face grew red with anger and green with envy. She stood still for a moment and then she hissed, "Yes, yes, I have a plan!"

The wicked woman remembered the words of an evil magician who had told her that the secret to lasting youth was to eat the heart and liver of a young and beautiful girl.
"Huntsman! Huntsman!" she screamed, "Come here at once!"

The vile stepmother ordered the huntsman to take Snow White deep into the forest and kill her. “Be sure to bring me back her heart and liver!” she instructed, “Or it will be the worst for you!”

The huntsman looked for Snow White and found her outside the masjid, placing her Qur’an in her bag. He watched as Snow White walked towards the forest picking some flowers. He looked around to see if anyone was near. He then took out his bow and arrow.

Suddenly, Snow White turned and saw the huntsman walking towards her.
"Child, I have been ordered by your stepmother to kill you," said the huntsman.
"Huntsman," cried Snow White, "please don't kill me!" She pleaded and pleaded with the huntsman to spare her life; in return she promised she would run far, far away and never again return to her home.

But the huntsman would not listen. "If I do not bring back your heart and liver, your wicked stepmother will kill me!" he said.
Tears fell from Snow Whites eyes as she raised her hands in prayer and recited the words of Prophet Noah. "Dear Allah, '*I am defeated: help me!*'[2]"

The huntsman took steps towards Snow White and raised his bow. As he moved closer he saw a boar approaching. He quickly aimed at the boar and killed it!
"Now I do not have to kill you," he said. "Instead I will take the heart and liver of the boar and deliver it to your wicked stepmother."
The huntsman hung his head in sorrow and relief and said, "You must run far away and never return. Your stepmother is an evil, sinful soul and will not rest until you are dead."

Snow White ran as fast as she could. Filled with fear she ran deeper and deeper into the forest. She held her Qur'an tightly in her arms. She tried hard not to cry, but she was all alone. "Help me dear Allah," cried Snow White. "I'm so afraid." Snow White knelt down and put her head on the ground and made *sujud.* "Dear Allah," she whispered, "You are *As-Samee*, The All-Hearing, please hear my call; You are *Al-Hafeez*, The Protector, please protect me; You are *Al-Fattah*, The Opener, please open a way for me."

After Snow White finished her *du'a*, she felt at peace. Snow White walked, and ran, for a long time. She stopped to make *tayammum* and then offered her prayers.

The moon shone brightly as Snow White continued her journey. Her hands, feet and face were deeply scratched and bruised from where she had fallen and brushed against thorns and thistles.

Finally she saw a cottage. She ran eagerly towards it, hoping to find help. She knocked on the door. Nobody opened it. She knocked again. The door remained closed. She knocked very loudly a third time, still nobody came, so Snow White lay down next to the door, holding her Qur'an tightly in her arms. Very soon she fell fast asleep.

Late into the night, a song could be heard.

"Allah! Allah! To You all praise we give,
Each step we take we think of You,
Allah, Allah, Allah, Allah ..."

The owners of the cottage were returning. They were seven dwarf sisters-in-faith who worked in the fields beyond the forest. As they arrived at the cottage, they saw Snow White lying asleep on the ground. The dwarfs were astonished.
"*La hawla wa la quwwata illa-billah,*" said one.
"What is this child doing in the forest by herself," asked a second.
"*Subhanallah,*" said a third.
"*Astaghfirullah*" said another, "Someone has harmed this child."
"*La ilaha ill-Allah*" said the strongest dwarf, and she came forward and gently picked up the sleeping child, taking her inside. Another covered her with a blanket.

Snow White slept a long, deep sleep. It wasn't until the next day when Snow White heard the call to prayer that she began to stir.

When she saw the dwarfs she quickly sat up filled with fear.

"Sweet child," they asked, "What is your name?"

Snow White was trembling. She could barely say her name. "Snow White," whispered the poor girl.

"What are you doing here?" asked the eldest dwarf.

Snow White was too afraid to speak. The dwarfs sensed that Snow White was alarmed.

One of the dwarfs came a little closer to Snow White. She had a wide smile.
"My name is Atifa the kind," she said, "please don't be afraid. These are my sisters.
This is our home."

The dwarf introduced Snow White to her sisters one by one.
"This is Batrisiya the wise. She is knowledgeable about many things, *mashallah.*
And this is Basilah the brave, she is strong, and has courage. Over there is Gufran
the forgiving, she is compassionate. Sitting on the chair is Adla the just, she is
honest and fair. Next to her is Karima the generous, who has a very charitable heart.
Sabira the patient is finishing her prayers. She never complains and she recites
Qur'an beautifully."

Snow White began to feel better. She was in a place where there was kindness, wisdom,
courage, forgiveness, honesty, generosity and patience. Slowly, Snow White began to
lose her fear. After a while she told the dwarfs how her stepmother wanted her dead
and how the huntsman had spared her life; how she had made her way through the
forest frightened and alone, and how she had stumbled on the cottage.

The dwarfs spoke amongst themselves and then said, "Dear Child, you can stay
here with us. We will give you shelter and food and make sure that no harm comes
to you." And so it was decided that Snow White would live with the dwarfs in comfort
and security.

Snow White spent her time doing many different things with the dwarfs. She loved to decorate using calligraphy with Gufran the forgiving. She made herbal medicines with Batrisiya the wise.

She would recite Qur'an with Sabira the patient. Sometimes she would go into the forest with Atifa the kind to help injured animals.

Once a month, Basilah the Brave would take her to the bazaar to sell her herbal medicines and calligraphy art.

Snow White was very content. She no longer had reason to be lonely or afraid. She lived happily with the dwarfs.

Years passed by, and Snow White had mastered all that the dwarfs had taught her.

One day, the wicked stepmother decided to question the *jinn* about her beauty, something she hadn't done in a very long time. "*Jinn, jinn,* obey my call.
Who is the fairest of them all?" she said.
The *jinn* replied, "O Lady, you are beautiful, fine and fair, but to Snow White's beauty you will never compare."

The stepmother fell to the ground in shock. Her eyes were filled with anger and hate. The stepmother knew that the *jinn* did not lie. She soon realised that the huntsman had deceived her. She began to pace up and down her chamber. What could she do to get rid of Snow White once and for all? The cruel and jealous stepmother soon came up with a wicked, wicked plan.

"Yes," hissed the stepmother, "It is the month of Ramadan, I will give poisoned dates to Snow White to break her fast and then, at last, she will die. And I will be the fairest of them all!"

Through her magic, the stepmother discovered that Snow White was living in a forest with seven dwarfs.

The stepmother crept down into her secret chamber.
She made a poisoned potion and sprinkled it on some dates.

The stepmother disguised herself as an old peddler woman.
She travelled to the cottage of the dwarfs. She waited until
it was almost time to break the fast. Then she knocked on
the door.

Snow White leaned out of a window and greeted her,
"*As-salamu 'alaykum.*"
"*Wa 'alaykum as-salam*, my dear," said
the stepmother. "Let me come inside,
I have some tasty dates to show you."
"*Jazaki Allahu khayran*, I'm sorry, but I've
been forbidden to let anyone in," answered Snow White.

The girl paused for a moment, then she said, "But it is commanded in the Qur'an to
'*render to the kindred their due rights, as (also) to those in want, and to the wayfarer*'[3].
So please help yourself to this water and food since it is almost time to break the fast."
Snow White reached out of the window and gave the disguised stepmother a jug of
water and food wrapped in a napkin.

“Oh never mind!” said the evil stepmother as she took the food and water, “I don’t need to come in. Here, take these delicious dates to break your fast.” The stepmother stretched out her arm to hand Snow White some dates.
But the girl hesitated.

“I’m so sorry,” said Snow White, “but I’ve been told that I’m not to accept things from strangers.”
“Oh they’re just dates,” said the stepmother, “after all it’s wrong to refuse dates during Ramadan.”
Snow White wasn’t sure what to do. “Very well,” she said, “I will take them to break my fast, *inshallah*, God will reward you for the gift.”

The stepmother pretended to walk away but instead she hid behind some trees and waited for Snow White to break her fast. She watched Snow White make *du'a* and pick up a date and look at it. "Yes, my beauty!" hissed the stepmother, "Now take a bite!"

As soon as Snow White took a bite, she fell to the ground.

The stepmother screeched a loud, evil laugh. "Now you will fall into a deep sleep and never awake!"

As the dwarfs were returning home, they saw a woman running through the woods laughing and shrieking, “Sleep, sleep and never wake! Never wake!”
“Listen! Listen!” cried Basilah the brave, “It must be Snow White’s stepmother!”
Basilah immediately ran after the stepmother but was only able to catch a glimpse of the stepmother’s face as she threw off her disguise and disappeared behind a thick grove of trees.

The other dwarfs reached the cottage and saw Snow White lying on the floor.
She was breathing but wouldn't wake up.
"The wicked stepmother poisoned our beautiful child," wept Sabira.

The dwarfs took turns to take care of Snow White. Days turned into weeks, weeks turned into months, and still Snow White slept.

One day, it so happened that a prince came riding by.
"*As-salamu 'alaykum*," said the prince.
"*Wa 'alaykum as-salam*," answered Karima.
"Respected grandmother," he said, "may I have a drink from your well?"
"*Inshallah*, my son," said the dwarf. "Let me get you some food to eat as well."

When the prince finished his drink he saw Snow White with the Qur'an on her lap, but her eyes were closed and she looked pale. He turned to Karima and asked, "Is she ill?" Karima sighed and nodded sadly. The other dwarfs came out and greeted the prince. One by one they told him about Snow White.
"She had the most beautiful voice when she recited Qur'an," wept Sabira.
"She would carry her Qur'an everywhere, it was a gift from her mother," said Adla.
"I used to take her to the bazaar once a month," sighed Basilah. "She would just give away her medicine to the sick and her calligraphy to the needy."
"She would go to the forest and look for injured animals," said Atifa.
"She was as patient as Job, as peaceful as dawn, with a heart as pure as snow," sniffed Karima.

The Prince dropped to his knee and held up his hands. He recited the *Fatiha* and then said, "Take away the disease, O Lord of the people!" The prince blew the *du'a* on Snow White. The Prince then said that he would send his mother, the Queen, to visit Snow White.

A few days later the Queen arrived with a doctor to examine Snow White. She then made a cordial from rare and special herbs, honey and black seed oil. The doctor said *bismillah* and recited the *Fatiha*. She placed the drink near Snow White's lips. The herb drink trickled into Snow White's mouth.

Every day the doctor gave Snow White more of the cordial. Every day Snow White stirred a little, until one day she opened her eyes. "*La ilaha ill-Allah*," were the first words she whispered.

The dwarfs cried with happiness. The Prince's mother was informed about the wonderful news. She came immediately and asked the dwarfs whether they would permit Snow White to marry her son. The dwarfs presented Snow White with the proposal. Although the dwarfs did not want Snow White to leave, they wanted her to be safe and happy. Snow White consented, and the dwarfs gave their blessing and prepared to attend the wedding.
"*Inshallah*, she will always be happy and safe with us," said the Queen.

The King and Queen invited many people to the wedding; one of the guests was Snow White's wicked stepmother.

On the day of the wedding, the stepmother put on her finest dress and jewels. When she was finished she said, "*Jinn, jinn,* obey my call. Who is the fairest of them all?"

The *jinn* replied, "O Lady, you are beautiful, fine and fair, but to the soon-to-be Princess Snow White you will never compare."

"What?" gasped the evil stepmother, "Snow White? Still alive? And a princess? I must put an end to her once and for all!" The wicked woman screamed as she ran down the steps to her secret chamber.

In her secret chamber the Stepmother boiled and stirred, added and measured, until finally her poisonous potion was ready. She took a comb and dipped it into the ghastly venom.

The people had gathered from all over the kingdom for the wedding feast. One of the first to arrive was the stepmother. Basilah the brave was standing near one of the entrances and recognised the stepmother. "No it cannot be!" gasped Basilah. "She is here!"
Basilah rushed towards the evil woman and grabbed her arm.
"You will not harm our Snow White a second time!"
The stepmother peered menacingly at the dwarf. "I have come to give my blessings, not to do harm."
"You must come with me," said Basilah.
"Very well," said the stepmother.
As they were walking down a corridor, the wicked stepmother pushed Basilah into a room and locked it. The stepmother quickly disguised herself as a housekeeper. Then she hurried to Snow White's room where the dwarfs were helping the new bride prepare for the wedding.

"Princess, the Queen has sent me to comb your hair," lied the stepmother.
"How kind," said Snow White, as she sat down on a chair in front of a large mirror.

The stepmother stood behind Snow White with the comb raised high. But she could not prevent herself from gazing into the mirror. She noticed that her own hair was out of place while Snow White's was neatly set. So vain was the wicked woman, that without thinking she ran the comb through her own hair. In an instant she fell to the ground.

"*Subhanallah*," cried Snow White. "It's my stepmother!" Snow White immediately removed the poisonous comb from her stepmother's head. With the help of the dwarfs she carried her to a bed. A doctor was summoned.

After the stepmother was attended to, the wedding celebrations continued. Snow White and the prince were married amidst tears of happiness, shouts of laughter and grand festivity.

After many days of treatment the stepmother opened her eyes. She was shocked to see Snow White with a crown on her head, sitting beside her.
"What are you going to do to me?" asked the stepmother, awaiting a great punishment.
"I shall forgive you, as Allah has commanded forgiveness," answered Snow White.
The stepmother looked at Snow White in disbelief. Snow White recited a verse from Qur'an,

but forgive them, and overlook (their misdeeds): for Allah loves those who are kind.[4]

"But I have done many terrible things," murmured the stepmother.
Snow White responded by saying,

those who afterwards repent and mend their ways–Allah is most forgiving and merciful.[5]

The stepmother recovered from the poison and they say she never again looked in a mirror.

As for Snow White, the Prince and the seven dwarfs, they all lived happily ever after.

The Daybreak

Say: I seek refuge with the Lord of the Dawn

From the mischief of created things;

From the mischief of Darkness
as it overspreads;

From the mischief of those who practise
secret arts;

And from the mischief of the envious
one as he practices envy.[6]

GLOSSARY

Al-Hafeez – A name or attribute of God: The Protector, The Guardian, The Preserver.
Al-Fattah – A name or attribute of God: The Opener, The Granter of Success, The Revealer.
As-salamu 'alaykum; wa 'alaykum as-salam – 'Peace be with you'/'And on you be peace'.
As-Samee – A name or attribute of God: The All-Hearing, the Ever-Listening.
Astaghfirullah – 'I ask God's forgiveness'.
Bismillah – 'In the name of God'.
Du'a – Supplication; personal prayer.
Fatiha – The opening chapter of the Qur'an.
Inshallah – 'God-willing'.
Jazaki Allahu khayran – 'May God reward your goodness' (feminine grammatical form).
Jinn – A being created from smokeless fire, living in an alternate dimension on earth.
La hawla wa la quwwata illa-billah – 'There is no power or strength but from God'.
La ilaha ill-Allah – 'There is no god but Allah.' The Islamic declaration of faith.
Mashallah – 'God has willed it'; said when admiring something or someone.
Masjid – A building for worship and learning.
Ramadan – A month in the Islamic calendar, fasting also occurs in this month.
Subhanallah – 'Glory be to God.'
Sujud – Prostration with one's head on the ground, as performed during the ritual prayer.
Tayammum – Dry ablution, performed when there is no water.